Can Do, Jenny Archer

Can Do, Jenny Archer

by Ellen Conford

Illustrated by Diane Palmisciano

Little, Brown and Company

Boston   New York   Toronto   London

To Susan Beth Pfeffer,
because she never lets me say, "Can't do."

Text copyright © 1991 by Conford Enterprises Ltd.
Illustrations copyright © 1991 by Diane Palmisciano

First Paperback Edition

The characters and events in this book are fictitious. Any similarity to real
persons, living or dead, is coincidental and not intended by the author.

Library of Congress Cataloging-in-Publication Data

Conford, Ellen.
    Can do, Jenny Archer / by Ellen Conford ; illustrated by
Diane Palmisciano. — 1st ed.
        p.   cm.
    Summary: In attempting to win a can-collecting contest, the winner of which
will direct a class movie, Jenny risks losing her best friend.
    ISBN 0-316-15356-7 (hc)
    ISBN 0-316-15372-9 (pb)
    [1. Friendship — Fiction.   2. Schools — Fiction.] I. Palmisciano, Diane,
ill.   II. Title. PZ7.C7593Can   1991
    [Fic] — dc20   91-9012

10 9 8 7 6

COM-MO

Published simultaneously in Canada
by Little, Brown & Company (Canada) Limited

PRINTED IN THE UNITED STATES OF AMERICA

1

"I have some exciting news, class," said Mrs. Pike.

It was almost lunchtime, and Jenny Archer was starving. She drew a piece of apple pie in her notebook. Sometimes Mrs. Pike's exciting news wasn't very exciting.

Once, Mrs. Pike had said it would be exciting to watch a film strip called *Tommy Tooth and the Whole Truth About Teeth*. But it wasn't.

She had said it would be exciting to study

how wheat is turned into bread. But it wasn't.

Jenny drew a scoop of ice cream on the apple pie.

"We're going to have a contest," said Mrs. Pike.

Jenny put down her pencil. She pushed her glasses back on her nose.

"The whole school will take part," Mrs. Pike went on. "We're going to collect empty tin cans to sell to a scrap-metal dealer. We'll use the money to buy a video camcorder and a TV monitor for the school."

"What kind of a contest is that?" asked Clifford Stern. "Just collecting cans?"

"The class that collects the most cans," said Mrs. Pike, "will use the camera first. We will make our own class movie. You could all be stars!"

Me, a movie star! Jenny thought. Now, that was exciting. She pictured herself accepting an Academy Award. She would say, "It

2

all started when I was in a little school . . ."

"The person in the class who brings in the most cans will direct the first movie," Mrs. Pike finished.

Wow! Directing a movie might be even better than starring in one. The director could make up the whole story. She would choose the actors and tell everybody what to do. Jenny loved to make up stories. And she was good at telling people what to do.

She was sure she'd be a great director.

The whole class was buzzing now. Jenny forgot she was starving. She looked over at her friend Beth. Beth's eyes were bright. She thought this was a great idea, too.

"You can be the star of my movie," Jenny whispered to her.

"What do you mean, *your* movie?" Beth asked.

"When I win the contest," Jenny said.

"What if *I* win the contest?" Beth said.

3

"But I have to win," answered Jenny. "I've always wanted to make a movie."

"Since when?"

"Well, I just realized it now," Jenny admitted. "But don't you think I'd make a good director?"

"I think *I* might make a good director," Beth said. "Why should you be the director?"

Beth was one of Jenny's two best friends. Jenny didn't want to fight with her. But she really wanted to win this contest. She just had to direct the class movie.

Yet, someday, when she was a famous moviemaker, she would still want Beth to be her friend.

"Let's not fight," Jenny said. "We'd both be good directors."

"You're right." Beth grinned. "We won't fight. Let's just say, may the best can collector win."

Jenny shook Beth's hand. "May the best can collector win," she repeated.

As long as it's me, she told herself.

2

Mrs. Butterfield was waiting for Jenny when she got home that afternoon. Mrs. Butterfield stayed with Jenny when Mr. and Mrs. Archer were at work.

"Your mother left me a shopping list," she said. "We'll have to get some groceries."

"Great!" Jenny said.

Mrs. Butterfield looked puzzled. Jenny liked food. But she wasn't crazy about shopping for it.

The supermarket is full of cans, Jenny

thought. Shelves and shelves of cans.

"We need a lot of stuff," she said.

When they got to the store Mrs. Butterfield checked her list. "Chicken." They pushed their shopping cart toward the meat counter.

"And tomato sauce," Jenny added as she pointed to a stack of cans. "Look. Five for a dollar. That's a good sale. We'd better get five."

"Your mother didn't put tomato sauce on the list," Mrs. Butterfield said.

"She must have forgotten it," said Jenny. "She always uses it to make Chicken Italiano."

"Well, all right." Mrs. Butterfield put a can in the cart. Jenny added four more cans.

"She certainly doesn't need five cans for one chicken," Mrs. Butterfield said.

"But they're on *sale*," said Jenny.

"I'm sure two cans are plenty," said Mrs. Butterfield firmly.

Oh, well, Jenny thought. I've only just begun to shop.

Mrs. Butterfield took a package of frankfurters and dropped them in the cart. Right above the meat counter was a row of canned sauerkraut.

"Sauerkraut," Jenny said. "For the franks."

"It's not on the list."

"But you can't have frankfurters without sauerkraut!" Jenny said. "She must have forgotten to write it down."

"Maybe," said Mrs. Butterfield. She put a can of sauerkraut in the cart.

They started down the canned vegetable and fruit section. Jenny had never noticed how many different kinds of vegetables came in cans.

"What's kale?" she asked.

"It's like spinach," said Mrs. Butterfield. "Only greener."

"Let's get some."

"You don't like spinach," Mrs. Butterfield reminded her.

"That's probably because it isn't green enough," Jenny said.

"We are not buying any kale." Mrs. Butterfield put the can back on the shelf. "Why are you suddenly so interested in kale?"

"I'm not so interested in kale," Jenny said. "I'm interested in cans." She told Mrs. Butterfield about the contest.

"If it's on the list and it comes in a can, I'll buy it," said Mrs. Butterfield. "Otherwise, you'll have to ask your mother."

They reached the end of the vegetable aisle.

"Look!" Jenny saw a big shopping cart piled high with cans. There was a big sign over it. 39¢ EACH!!!

"Wow! What a good sale!" Jenny started poking through the cans.

"Fruit cocktail! I love fruit cocktail! Corn! I love corn! Potted meat product! I love —"

10

Mrs. Butterfield grabbed her hand. "You don't even know what potted meat product is."

"Who cares?" said Jenny. "It's only thirty-nine cents. Thirty-nine little cents. *Please*, Mrs. Butterfield. I know my mother would let me buy some cans."

"All right." Mrs. Butterfield gave in. "Take four cans. But no more."

They were almost at the end of the list.

"Dog food," Jenny read. She ran ahead to the pet food section. Barkley always ate Bow Wow Burgers with Bacon Bits. But they came in a box.

And Jenny saw there were shelves and shelves of canned pet food.

By the time Mrs. Butterfield reached her, Jenny had an armful of cans.

"Barkley doesn't eat any of those," said Mrs. Butterfield.

"I know," said Jenny. "Don't you think he's

12

bored with Bow Wow Burgers by now?"

Mrs. Butterfield threw up her hands. "Pick four cans of dog food and let's get out of here."

"Okay." Jenny picked out four different kinds of dog dinners. She had eleven cans all together. A very good start.

She pushed the cart toward the checkout counter. At the counter she noticed a little basket full of cans. The cans had pictures of tiny oranges on the labels.

"Kumquats!" Jenny read. "I love —"

"No!" said Mrs. Butterfield. "Absolutely, positively *no kumquats*."

"All right." Jenny started to unload the shopping cart.

"Boy, this was fun!" she said. "Let's go shopping again tomorrow."

Mrs. Butterfield put her hand over her eyes as if she had a headache.

"Let's not," she said.

3

That night Jenny told her parents about the contest. She explained about the fruit cocktail and the new dog foods and the potted meat product.

"I don't know what potted meat product is," she said. "But it was only thirty-nine cents."

"Nobody knows what it is," her father said. "Maybe Barkley will like it."

"It's not dog food," said Jenny.

"Well, it's not my idea of people food," her father said.

*　*　*

The next morning Jenny met Beth and Wilson at the corner of Lemon Street.

"I have four cans already," Jenny said. "How many do you two have?"

"I don't have any," Beth answered. "We ate out last night."

"That's too bad." But Jenny secretly hoped the Moores would eat out a lot this month.

"My mother microwaves a lot," Wilson said. "She gets a lot of stuff in plastic."

"That's a shame," Jenny said. Thank goodness the Archers didn't have a microwave.

"You don't really mean that, Jenny," Beth said. "You're glad we don't have any cans yet."

"No, I'm not," said Jenny. She wouldn't mind if Wilson and Beth had collected a couple of cans. As long as they didn't have as many as she had.

"You are, too," Beth said.

Wilson looked from one girl to the other. "Are you fighting?" he asked, worried.

"No," said Jenny. She waited for Beth to agree that they weren't fighting.

But Beth didn't say anything.

And Jenny began to worry, too.

4

That afternoon Beth went shopping for shoes. Wilson had to go to the doctor with his mother and his baby brother, Tyler.

So Jenny was alone as she walked home from school. She was still worried.

Beth had talked to her in school. But she hadn't talked much. Jenny couldn't understand why Beth should be mad at her.

Just because they both wanted to win the contest it didn't mean they had to be enemies.

As she walked up Lemon Street she noticed something that made her forget all about Beth.

In front of every house on the block there was a blue plastic trash can.

It was recycling day! Every Tuesday everyone put out all their bottles and cans in the blue plastic containers. The garbage collectors picked them up in the afternoon.

There must be hundreds of cans in those containers, Jenny thought. If she could get to them before the garbage collectors came —

She dashed up the block and ran into her house.

Barkley came to meet her at the door.

"Plastic bags!" she shouted. "I need plastic bags! *Big* ones!"

She ran into the kitchen and reached under the sink. She pulled out a box of trash bags. Barkley danced around her excitedly.

"What do you need those for?" asked Mrs. Butterfield.

"To win the contest!"

Jenny raced out of the house with Barkley on her heels.

She ran to the driveway next door. She pulled the lid off the blue container. Barkley poked his head inside. He loved looking through garbage cans.

"Nothing for you, Barkley," said Jenny. She pushed bottles aside and dug through the container. Six cans! She tossed them into her plastic bag and ran to the next house.

Barkley trotted after her. He couldn't figure out what she was doing. But every time she opened a container, he looked inside hopefully.

Jenny didn't notice as the Moore's car pulled up in front of their house.

"*Jenny Archer!*" Beth shrieked. "What are

you doing in our garbage?"

Jenny jumped. Barkley ran to greet Beth. Beth didn't even stop to pet him.

"I'm just — um —" Jenny didn't want to share her great idea. "Did you get nice shoes?"

"I know what you're doing! Mom!"

Mrs. Moore looked confused. "What's going on?"

Beth raced to her front door. "I need trash bags!" she yelled. "Fast!"

5

Jenny started to run back down Lemon Street. But she had to carry her bag of cans with her. They banged against her leg and slowed her down.

Beth zoomed out of her house carrying a plastic bag.

Jenny ran faster. As she headed down Lemon Street, Beth ran the other way and turned the corner.

She was smart. Instead of getting into a

race with Jenny on the same block, Beth was starting on a new street.

Mr. Munch's street!

Mr. Munch had a huge Great Dane named Millicent. She probably ate fifty cans of dog food a week.

Jenny made a run for Mr. Munch's house.

Millicent was sitting on the front steps.

Jenny pulled the lid off Mr. Munch's blue container. Millicent stood up and barked.

"I'm collecting cans," Jenny explained.

"Woof!" Millicent trotted down the steps toward Jenny.

Barkley placed himself in front of Jenny.

Jenny loved dogs. But Millicent was very big.

"I'm not stealing anything," Jenny said.

"*Woof!*" said Millicent.

"Arf!" Barkley barked back at the Great Dane. He knew he should protect Jenny.

But he didn't look too eager to argue with Millicent.

Mr. Munch came down the steps.

"I'm collecting cans for school," Jenny told him. "Is it okay if I take yours? I thought you'd have a lot of dog food cans."

"Go ahead," said Mr. Munch. He put his hand on Millicent's collar. "But Millicent eats Hungry Hound Chow. We buy it in twenty-five-pound bags. Do you need any bags?"

"No," said Jenny. "Just cans."

"Too bad. But you can take what's there."

There were only five cans in the bin. She put them in her plastic bag. She'd wasted a lot of time here. Beth was already at the last house on the other end of the block.

"Thanks anyway," Jenny said, disappointed.

She heard a rumbling noise behind her. The garbage truck was just turning onto the street.

"Oh, no!" She started to run, dragging the plastic bag behind her. Now she was in a double race. Not just with Beth, but with the garbage collectors, too.

She ran to the next house. She ripped the lid off the recycling bin. She reached inside and grabbed three cans.

As fast as she could, she made her way down the block. The garbage collectors were right behind her. Jenny reached the end of the block ahead of the truck. Her bag was getting heavy. She turned the corner.

Barkley hung back a little.

"Come on, Barkley," she said.

Barkley lowered his head. He eyed the bulging trash bag. For a moment he stood absolutely still.

Then, letting out a loud "*Arf!*" he pounced on it.

"No!" yelled Jenny. "What are you doing?"

She tugged at the bag. Barkley jumped on it again.

"Stop that! This isn't a game!"

But Barkley thought it was. He barked happily as the bag split open. Cans spilled out all over the sidewalk.

"Oh, Barkley!" Jenny wailed. "Look what you've done!"

Just then the garbage truck pulled to a stop in front of her.

"Hey, kid!" One of the garbage collectors jumped off the truck. He glared at her angrily. "Look at the mess you're making."

"Don't touch them!" Jenny cried. "I'll pick them all up."

The plastic bag was in shreds. Cans clattered all over the sidewalk. They tumbled into the gutter. Barkley was swatting cans with his nose and chasing after the ones that rolled away.

The garbage man scowled at her. "What are you trying to do? Make our job harder?"

Jenny looked around at the trash explosion Barkley had set off. "I know you're not going to believe this," she said. "But I was trying to make it easier."

6

Jenny didn't often run out of ideas, but a week later she was stumped.

Barkley didn't like any of the canned dog food Jenny bought. Her parents were getting tired of making casseroles out of canned soup. The Moores hadn't eaten out in seven days. And all the kids in the neighborhood were collecting cans. When recycling day came again, there wasn't a can to be found in any of the blue bins.

There were only two weeks to go in the

contest. And Jenny had only one bag of cans so far.

On Sunday the Archers went to visit Jenny's grandparents. They lived in an apartment house called Boxwood Gardens.

Jenny always loved visiting them. But she was looking forward to the visit more than usual today. She had told them about the contest. They'd promised to save all their empty cans for her. She wondered how many cans they had collected.

"Wait till you see, Jenny," Grandpa said when she came in. "We have two whole bags of cans for you."

"Wow!" Jenny couldn't believe it. Grandpa and Grandma didn't even have a dog. "You must have eaten a lot of kale," she said.

"I asked my friends to save their cans for you, too," Grandma said. She opened the cabinet under the sink. She pulled out two

white plastic bags. But they were little ones. The size that fit into wastebaskets.

"Oh." Jenny felt a wave of disappointment. She had been picturing great big trash bags, bulging with cans. These were so small.

"What's the matter?" asked Grandpa. "I thought you'd be pleased. We ate an awful lot of Noodle Doodles for lunch this week."

"What in the world are Noodle Doodles?" asked Mrs. Archer.

"Don't ask," said Grandma. "He discovered them in the supermarket. They're round. With cream sauce."

"I'll bet they're from the same company that makes potted meat product," said Mr. Archer.

"We haven't lived here too long," Grandpa said. "We only asked the people we know."

"Thank you," Jenny said. "Really. It's just — I was sort of thinking of bigger bags."

"Let's have some coffee and cake," Grandma said. "You'll like the cake, Jenny. I used canned frosting."

While the grown-ups chatted, Jenny thought about the contest. She thought about Boxwood Gardens. It was three floors high, with apartments on every floor.

Her grandparents had only asked their friends for cans. But other people might want to help if they knew about the contest.

Jenny twisted a strand of hair around her finger.

Maybe she could go from door to door and ask everyone if they had empty cans.

No, she told herself. Her parents wouldn't want her to go around to strange people's apartments.

If there was some way she could tell everyone in the building about the contest —

And suddenly she had a great idea.

7

In the basement of the apartment house there was a big bulletin board. There were always signs on it about activities and clubs. There were ads from people who wanted to buy or sell things.

She could put up a CANS WANTED sign. Everyone in the building would see it. Then, next week, she could come back and pick up the cans. With everyone in the building collecting cans for her, by next weekend she'd have enough to fill a garbage truck!

Grandma gave her a piece of paper and a

black marking pen. Jenny worked at the kitchen table. The grown-ups went to visit the neighbors in the next apartment.

When she finished her sign, she found a box of large trash bags under the sink. She pulled out two. She ran downstairs to the basement, much too excited to wait for the elevator.

She ran toward the laundry room. She nearly bowled over two women carrying laundry baskets. One woman was very tall. The other had bright red, curly hair.

"Whose little girl are you?" asked the red-haired woman.

"I'm Jenny Archer. My grandparents live here. Is it okay if I put a sign on the bulletin board?"

"Go right ahead," the woman said. "That's what it's there for."

Jenny stood on tiptoe. She put her sign right in the middle of the bulletin board. She

35

shook open the plastic bags and tacked them under the sign.

"This certainly looks like a worthy cause," the tall woman said.

"Oh, it is." Jenny nodded.

"And what a clever sign," the woman added.

"What a good idea," said the tall woman. "I'll be glad to help."

"So will I," said the red-haired woman.

Jenny smiled her thanks. The sign hadn't even been up one minute. And already she had two contributors.

And if everyone in Boxwood Gardens was this nice . . . she'd bring in more cans than her whole class put together!

Maybe she'd make her first film about the contest.

She could call it *Can Do, Jenny Archer.*

And if Beth was still angry at her, she'd star in it herself.

8

Jenny didn't look for new ways to collect cans that week. She did save all the cans from Barkley's dog food. And she saved all the tomato sauce and vegetable cans from dinner.

But her grandfather had told her there were twelve apartments on each floor of his building. Even if she got only five cans from each apartment — five times twelve was sixty cans a floor. Times three was a hundred eighty cans!

Jenny stopped worrying about having

enough cans. She began to worry that she wouldn't be able to fit them all into her parents' car.

Beth still walked to school with Jenny and Wilson. But ever since she'd caught Jenny at her recycling bin, Beth had acted cold.

Every time Jenny said, "We're still friends, right?" Beth nodded. But she didn't seem very friendly at all.

Wilson never talked about the contest. Maybe he thought that if he didn't talk about it, Jenny and Beth would stop thinking about it.

The next Saturday Jenny's father drove her to Boxwood Gardens. She couldn't wait to see how many cans had been donated.

She ran down to the basement ahead of her father. She raced to the bulletin board. But halfway down the hall, she could see that something was wrong.

There were no trash bags full of cans

waiting for her. Her sign was gone. In its place was a poster that read, ADORABLE KITTENS FOR ADOPTION.

"What happened?" Jenny cried. "Where's my sign? Where are my cans?"

"I have no idea," her father said. "Maybe Grandma and Grandpa know."

They took the elevator to the third floor. But Jenny's grandparents didn't know what had happened either.

"The bag was there when I did the laundry on Wednesday," Grandma said.

"I'll call the super," said Grandpa. "Maybe he's got them."

When Grandpa got off the phone, he was shaking his head. "The super threw them out. With the trash."

"Oh, no!" Jenny wailed. "Why did he do that?"

"He said he didn't see your sign. All he saw was a notice about kittens and a trash bag in the hall with cans falling out."

Someone had tacked ADORABLE KITTENS over Jenny's sign. What a mean thing to do.

"This is awful," Jenny said.

Grandma stroked Jenny's hair. "How about a piece of orange cake? My orange cake always cheers you up."

"Did you use canned frosting?" Jenny asked.

"I certainly did."

"I don't really like canned frosting," Jenny said. She tried not to cry. "And I'm not too crazy about kittens right now either."

9

On Monday morning, Jenny told Beth and Wilson what had happened at Boxwood Gardens. She didn't even worry that Beth might steal her great idea. She was sure she wouldn't win the contest now.

"What a shame," Beth said. She sounded as if she really meant it. "That was a smart idea."

"Except it didn't work," Jenny said sadly.

Suddenly she didn't feel so terrible. Beth could have been glad that her plan failed. Instead, she was sorry for her.

Keeping a good friend like Beth was more important than winning a contest, Jenny decided.

Of course, it would be nice if she could do both.

"How are you doing, Wilson?" Beth asked.

"Not bad," said Wilson.

"How many cans do you have?" she asked.

"I'm not sure," he said. "I haven't counted them."

"Well, I hope one of you wins," said Jenny, "since I'm not going to."

"You don't know that for sure," Beth said.

"Yes, I do," said Jenny. "Because I give up."

"That's not like you, Jenny," her mother said that night. "Giving up just because you had a little setback."

"It was a *big* setback," Jenny said. "A *giant* setback."

"But even if you don't win the contest,"

her father said, "you're earning money for the school."

"That's true." Jenny curled a strand of hair around her finger.

"And you still might win," her mother said. "Even without the cans from Boxwood Gardens."

"I don't know," said Jenny.

"Let's go to the supermarket," her father said.

Jenny was puzzled. "Again? We just went Saturday."

"I know," said her father. "But we're fresh out of potted meat product."

Jenny got up an hour early Tuesday morning. It was still dark out. She dressed fast. She tiptoed out of the house with Barkley following her.

She walked up Lemon Street silently. She stopped at all the houses where there were no children. She checked the recycling bins.

She felt almost like a spy. She could be looking for secret plans in the dead of night. Jenny Archer, Special Agent. Commander of the Tin Can Control Patrol.

She held her hand over her mouth to keep from giggling out loud. She didn't want anyone to hear her prowling around. They might call the police.

She collected eleven more cans.

The sun was rising as she made her way to Mr. Marvel's delicatessen. He sold a lot of take-out food. He made it himself. His blue bin was full of empty bottles. And seven cans.

I guess I shouldn't give up after all, Jenny thought. She was pleased with herself as she hurried home in the morning mist.

She'd found eighteen more cans.

And she still had two more days to win the contest.

10

"I think I'm turning into tin," said Jenny's mother. It was Thursday night. The Archers had been eating canned food all week. Peas, beans, sardines, fruit cocktail, ravioli, tuna. . . .

"Me, too," said Jenny's father. "Thank goodness this is over."

"You didn't like my dinner?" asked Mrs. Archer.

"Alphabet soup, chili, and French-fried

onion rings?" he said. "It was a new high in classy dining."

"I loved it," said Jenny.

"How many cans do you have?" her mother asked.

"I don't know," Jenny said. "I haven't counted them yet."

"What are you waiting for?" her father asked. "We have to bring them in tomorrow."

"I only have two and a half bags," Jenny said. "How long can that take?"

"Fifty-six, fifty-seven, fifty-eight . . ."

"Woof!"

"Not now, Barkley, I'm counting. Fifty-nine, sixty —"

"*Woof!*"

"I *can't* walk you now. Fifty-seven, fifty-eight — oh, no! Where was I?

"Rats! One, two, three . . ."

With her parents' help, Jenny finally fin-

ished counting at eight-thirty. She had one hundred seven cans.

"That doesn't sound like so many," she said. "Just think if I had all the cans from Boxwood Gardens."

"You worked hard, and you helped your school," her mother said. "That's more important than winning."

"But if winning isn't important," Jenny began, "why hold a contest?"

Her parents looked at each other. For a moment neither of them said anything.

Then:

"Bedtime!" her father said.

"No, it isn't," Jenny said.

"Not yours," he told her. "Mine."

"But it's only eight-thirty."

"I know." He grinned. "But it's going to take me all night to figure out an answer to your question."

11

Jenny couldn't wait to get to school on Monday. Everyone had brought in their cans on Friday and left them in the schoolyard. The scrap-metal dealer had weighed the cans over the weekend.

The principal would check the totals and announce the winner first thing in the morning.

Mrs. Pike had given out stick-on labels so everyone could put their names on their bags. Jenny had watched as other kids unloaded bags from their parents' cars.

Jenny had two and a half bags. They

weren't full, but most of the other kids didn't even have two.

It was a good thing she hadn't given up! She might win the contest after all.

Mrs. Grant's voice boomed over the p.a. system.

"And now, the news you've all been waiting for."

Jenny and Beth looked at each other excitedly. Beth hadn't told Jenny how many cans she had, and Jenny hadn't seen her come to school with them on Friday.

Jenny held out her hand. "Good luck," she told Beth. Beth squeezed Jenny's hand. "Good luck, Jenny."

"The winner is —" Suddenly Mrs. Grant laughed. Right over the loudspeaker. "And a good name for a winner it is! From Mr. Greenburg's class, Wilson Wynn!"

Wilson!

Jenny's mouth dropped open. She turned

to Beth. Beth looked even more surprised than Jenny.

"How did he do it?" Jenny asked. "He's only a little kid."

"I don't know," said Beth. "I don't understand it. I was sure you'd win, after I —" She stopped short.

"After you what?" Jenny asked.

"Nothing," Beth said.

"It is so something," Jenny insisted. "What did you do?"

"Well," said Beth, "on Friday I put your name on my label. So you'd get credit for my cans."

"You did?" Jenny stared at her friend. "Why?"

"Because I only had one bag," Beth said. "I couldn't win. But if I added mine to yours, you had more bags than anyone in our class."

"But you were mad at me," Jenny said. "Why did you want me to win?"

"You were so sad about what happened at your grandparents' house," Beth said. "I never heard you just quit like you did after that. You *never* give up."

For once, Jenny didn't know what to say. She had lost the contest. Yet all of a sudden she felt like the luckiest person in the world.

That afternoon Jenny and Beth waited for Wilson after school.

"Congratulations," Jenny said to him. "If we couldn't win, we're glad you did."

"Thank you," said Wilson. "I never won anything before in my whole life. You're not mad at me?"

"No, we're proud of you," Beth said.

"And we can help you direct your movie," Jenny said with a gleam in her eye. "Beth and I will be your assistant directors."

"Well, I don't know," Wilson said. "I think I'm supposed to —"

"I can't wait till you get the video camera," Jenny said excitedly.

"But where did you get all those cans?" Beth asked.

"My aunt's a veterinarian," Wilson said. "She has a kennel for boarding animals."

"Oh, I get it," said Jenny. "She must use a ton of pet food."

Wilson nodded. "It's a big kennel."

"That's really smart," Beth said. "I was sure Jenny would win."

"Beth gave me all her cans," Jenny told Wilson. "Wasn't that an amazing thing to do?"

"Oh, come on," Beth said shyly.

"You're a true friend," Wilson said.

"That's right," said Jenny. "And I'm never going to forget what you did, Beth. As long as I live."

"Don't be silly." Beth's cheeks turned pink.

"I'm not being silly," Jenny said. "Just wait and see. Wilson's movie is only the beginning."

"But I'm not sure —" Wilson began.

"Someday I'm going to be a famous director," Jenny went on. "And when I win the Academy Award, Beth Moore is going to be the first person I thank."

"What about me?" Wilson asked. "Aren't you going to thank me?"

"I'm going to thank you right now." She grabbed him and gave him a big hug.

"Ow!" he yelled. "Jenny, would you do me a favor?"

"Sure," she said. "What is it?"

Wilson rubbed his neck. "Don't thank me so hard."